OAK PARK PUBLIC LIBRARY ™

SPACE SCOUT

SCOUTING THE UNIVERSE FOR A NEW EARTH

The Slime Volcano
published in 2010 by
Hardie Grant Egmont
85 High Street
Prahran, Victoria 3181, Australia
www.hardiegrantegmont.com.au

PEFC
PEFC/21-31-16

*The pages of this book are printed on paper derived
from forests promoting sustainable management.*

A CiP record for this title is available from the National Library of Australia

Text copyright © 2010 H. Badger
Illustration and design copyright © 2010 Hardie Grant Egmont

Cover illustration by D. Mackie
Illustrated by D. Greulich and S. Spartels
Series design by S. Swingler
Typeset by Ektavo
Printed in Australia by McPherson's Printing Group

1 3 5 7 9 10 8 6 4 2

SPACE SCOUT™

THE SLIME VOLCANO

BY *H. BADGER*

ILLUSTRATED BY *D. GREULICH* AND *S. SPARTELS*

hardie grant EGMONT

CHAPTER 1

Why hasn't someone invented an easier way to do chores? Kip Kirby grumbled to himself. *After all, it IS the year 2354!*

Kip was twelve – old enough to stay home alone during the school holidays while his mum and dad were at work. But while they were away, Kip had to do chores around the apartment for his pocket money!

Kip was used to working hard, though. As well as going to school, he had a job as a Space Scout.

Space Scouts explored unknown galaxies in deep space. They were searching for Earth 2. The current Earth was running out of room, and another planet was needed for humans to live on. No other planet in the Milky Way had water or the right atmosphere.

Being a Space Scout was an honour, but a huge responsibility. Earth's future depended on Kip and the 49 other scouts.

Kip was due to leave for his next Space Scout mission in an hour!

In his apartment on the 2,342nd floor,

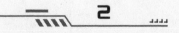

Kip squirted cleaning liquid onto the bathroom mirror. It was the latest Best-U model. Instead of showing your actual reflection, the Best-U suggested cool new hairstyles and outfits.

That day, Kip's reflection had short, blond hair with a blue spiky fringe. His outfit was a sparkling gold spacesuit.

Gold's my colour, Kip decided, imagining when he might get to wear a gold spacesuit for real.

The Shield of Honour presentation ceremony, he sighed. *If only…*

After finishing a mission, Space Scouts earned one Planetary Point. Important discoveries on new planets earned two

points. But the Space Scout who actually discovered the next Earth won the ultimate prize – the Shield of Honour.

Kip wanted to win it more than anything. He pictured himself holding up the shield while the other Space Scouts cheered. There were also other prizes for the winning Space Scout, like a brand-new Turbo RoboHorse to ride on Earth 2. Of course, saving humanity would be awesome, too.

Suddenly the doorbell rang, interrupting Kip's daydream. It was Jett, Kip's best friend from school. He lived on the 1,698th floor of Kip's apartment building.

'Check this out!' Jett grinned, holding a

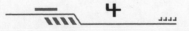

WorldCorp Turbo RoboHorse 8000

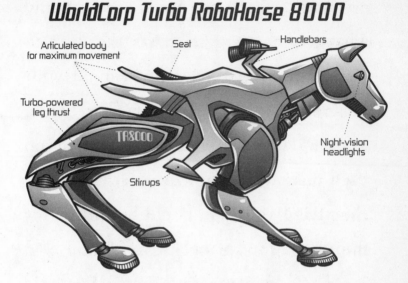

Articulated body
for maximum movement

Seat

Handlebars

Turbo-powered
leg thrust

TR8000

Night-vision
headlights

Stirrups

microphone with flashing blue and yellow lights.

'No way!' Kip said. 'Your parents got you a Pro-Planet Star Mic?'

Pro-Planet Star Mics were the latest craze at Kip and Jett's school. You simply sang into the microphone and it recorded

you, instantly adding backing vocals and a band.

The microphone then beamed your performance to big screens on Earth, Venus, Mars and Mercury. Local aliens on each planet voted on the best singers. If they liked you, you could be in line for immediate interplanetary fame!

'They love me on Venus,' Jett said modestly.

'Give me a go!' Kip begged.

Kip launched into one of his favourite hard rock songs, 'Space Junk'. Then Jett had a turn, singing 'Sun Spots'.

Next, Kip belted out a rocking version of 'Meteor Strike', with air guitar and

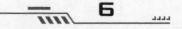

headbanging moves. But no matter what he did, Kip couldn't get the aliens watching on Mercury to vote for him.

'They must prefer boy bands on Mercury,' he muttered.

'Ewww,' Jett said. 'Gross!'

Then Kip remembered that he was *supposed* to be finishing his chores before he left on his next mission. He quickly flicked on his SpaceCuff.

SpaceCuffs were thick silver wrist cuffs with mini-supercomputers built in. Space Scouts used them to communicate with their starships on missions.

He checked the time. It was 16:58 hours already!

Kip had to leave for his mission in two minutes. A UniTaxi would be waiting for him on the roof of his apartment building to take him to his starship, MoNa 4000.

The Pro-Planet Star Mic had completely distracted Kip from his chores. His parents would kill him if he didn't finish them. Plus he'd miss out on his pocket money. All the same, he couldn't abandon the mission.

Saying a quick goodbye to Jett, Kip raced to his bedroom. He yanked on his spacesuit, which was bright green and custom-made to fit him perfectly.

His matching helmet had glittering flames on the side. Kip's space boots were brand new Cometchasers. According

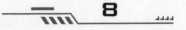

to gossip on the Space Scout intranet, Cometchasers were even better than Kip's old boots, the Hummingbird Pros.

It was time to leave.

I'll just have to do my chores when I get home, Kip decided. *Whenever that is!*

CHAPTER 2

Kip jumped into the lift outside his front door. The lift hurtled up a thousand floors in 0.2 seconds.

Kip raced onto the roof and spotted the waiting UniTaxi. It was green and pod-shaped, with a clear roof that opened automatically as Kip got closer.

He jumped inside and punched in

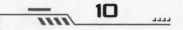

the co-ordinates for the Intergalactic Hoverport, where all space flights departed. The self-piloting UniTaxi rose into the air. In 2354, all spacecraft took off vertically. There wasn't room for runways on Earth.

The UniTaxi sped the 10 kilometres up to the Hoverport, where MoNa was docked.

Every cell in Kip's body buzzed with excitement. He loved heading into space. After all, not every kid got to explore unknown planets.

Soon, Kip could see the Hoverport looming up ahead. It looked like a giant car park floating in the air. But instead of old-fashioned cars, it had rows of starships.

Kip's starship was one of the biggest. MoNa was gleaming black with a pointed nosecone and powerful thrusters. She was custom-built for extreme long-distance space travel.

'Please open the landing bay door, MoNa,' Kip said into his SpaceCuff.

'NOW you decide to turn up?' said MoNa grumpily.

Kip rolled his eyes. *I'm not even that late!* he thought.

But he said nothing to MoNa. She was very bossy. Plus, she liked to think she knew everything about space travel. Kip preferred to ignore her bad moods.

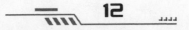

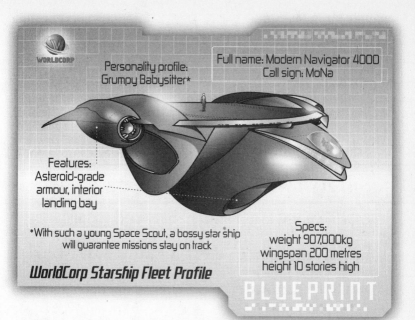

MoNa's external door slid open and the UniTaxi flew in. Kip leapt out into the landing bay.

'Welcome back!' said a friendly, growly voice. It was Finbar, Kip's second-in-command (or 2iC for short).

Finbar was part-human, part-arctic

wolf. He had fluffy white fur, ice-blue eyes and fangs peeping over his lips. He walked on two paws and towered over Kip.

You'd never know that Finbar is such a softie, Kip grinned to himself.

Finbar was an Animaul, bred to protect Earth in case of alien invasion. But he'd failed Animaul Basic Training for being too gentle. Finbar's wolf senses, agility and intelligence made him an ideal 2iC. Plus, Kip was plucky enough for both of them.

When not on missions with Kip, Finbar looked after MoNa.

Finbar looked exhausted. 'I've been cleaning MoNa all afternoon with my new Suckerbot,' he explained.

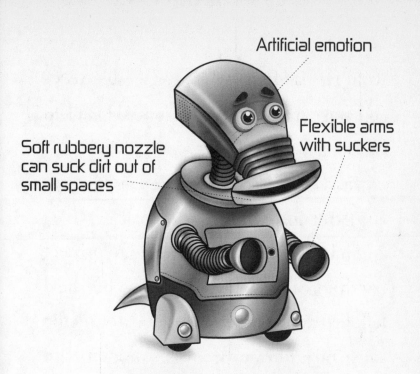

Artificial emotion

Soft rubbery nozzle can suck dirt out of small spaces

Flexible arms with suckers

WorldCorp Suckerbot

The Suckerbot was a cleaning robot with a nozzle shaped like lips. It could suck dirt out of the smallest corners.

It circled around Finbar making soft buzzing sounds. Kip could tell it was one of those clingy robots.

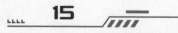

'Time for some real work now,' MoNa snorted. She saw and heard everything Kip and Finbar did.

Kip sighed. MoNa was impossible!

'Download your mission brief,' MoNa continued. 'I'll pilot us into space.'

'I thought *I* was captain of this starship,' Kip joked.

Still, he knew it made sense to let MoNa's autopilot handle the easy flying tasks. For more complicated flying, Kip's skills would be needed. He'd spent months in Space Scout training learning to fly a starship.

Kip and Finbar strode through the glowing blue corridors toward the bridge.

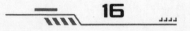

The bridge was MoNa's command centre.

The Suckerbot rolled along at Finbar's paws, slurping at them as he walked.

Located inside MoNa's nosecone, the bridge had two giant windows looking out to space. The floor was a lit-up map of the Milky Way.

Kip and Finbar took their seats in the middle of the room. Touching the air above his head, Kip activated his holographic consol.

A cylinder of blue light shot down, surrounding Kip and Finbar. MoNa's controls were projected on the cylinder.

Kip touched the 'Download Mission Brief' button in mid-air.

SPACE SCOUT KIP KIRBY MISSION BRIEF

Using its latest long-range intergalactic telescope, WorldCorp has discovered a new solar system. The largest planet has been named 'Grimor'.

Grimor has a single moon close by, just like Earth. This makes WorldCorp think Grimor could have Earth-like conditions.

A wormhole to Grimor will soon open.

Your mission:

Land on Grimor and work out if this unknown planet could be the next Earth.

Grimor, Kip echoed. *Doesn't exactly sound like paradise…*

Still, Grimor might be the answer to all of Earth's problems.

As well as my chance to win the Shield of Honour! thought Kip.

CHAPTER 3

When Kip looked out the window, he saw they'd left the Hoverport behind. A bright cloud mass swirled in the inky sky ahead. The wormhole to Grimor!

Wormholes were shortcuts between galaxies. Space Scouts used them to travel billions of light-years in seconds.

Kip took over MoNa's controls. He

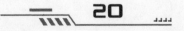

accelerated to warp speed and plunged the starship into the wormhole.

Instantly, Kip's guts felt like they were bursting through his skin. Travelling long distances that fast was tough.

They quickly popped out the other end of the wormhole. They were in a new galaxy, never visited by humans. Ahead lay a large, brown planet with patches of blue.

'Looks filthy,' Finbar murmured, smoothing down his whiskers.

The Suckerbot nuzzled at him, and Kip saw Finbar sneak him a handful of space-dust. Kip rolled his eyes.

'There's a lot of sulphur in the

atmosphere,' said MoNa, who'd taken the controls again. 'It's so dirty. I can't see a clear spot to aim the Scrambler Beams.'

Kip and Finbar travelled to the surface of each new planet via Scrambler Beam. The beams jumbled up Kip and Finbar's particles, shot them through space and put them back together on a planet's surface.

'I'll have to guess,' MoNa continued. 'Hope you don't land in anything yucky!'

Kip's training had prepared him for any situation. Gritting his teeth, he led the way back to the landing bay.

Kip stepped into a pair of footprints painted on the floor. Finbar stood on a pair of pawprints beside him. The Suckerbot

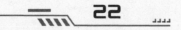

watched Finbar anxiously.

Two Scramblers shot down, and a nanosecond later, Kip and Finbar's particles were whizzing through space!

Kip opened his eyes. Finbar was beside him. Their particles had reassembled on Grimor.

Then Kip heard a little whirring sound. He glanced down. Finbar's Suckerbot was there too! He must have sneaked into his scrambler beam at the last minute.

'Er, Finbar,' Kip said, nudging him.

Finbar shrugged apologetically, but he also looked pleased. 'A cleaning robot will

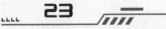

come in handy on this planet.'

Kip looked around. The surface of Grimor was a dingy brown-grey colour, with soaring craggy mountains covered in vines. There were pools of a strange, electric-blue slime everywhere, and the sky was a dim green colour.

The first thing Kip noticed was how heavy his body felt. Just lifting up his hand was harder than on Earth.

The gravitational force here must be stronger than on Earth, he guessed. *It feels like I weigh twice as much.*

The slime pools crawled with wriggling creatures as long as Kip's fingers. They looked like ugly centipedes, with lots of

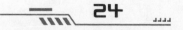

legs and thick shells outside their bodies.

The Suckerbot circled the pool, dying to suck up the slimy liquid. But just as it reached down with its nozzle-lips, one of the creatures snapped at it with dagger-sharp fangs.

The Suckerbot jumped back, cowering. Finbar scooped it up hurriedly. He didn't want his new robot getting damaged by alien creatures!

Kip shuddered. *Those little worm things are gross.*

Suddenly, he felt a weird rumbling under his feet. The air began to stink of toilets, even through Kip's helmet. A nearby mountain began to blow steam.

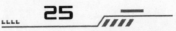

Hang on, thought Kip, *that's not a massive mountain. That's a —*

'Volcano!' Finbar yelled, clutching the Suckerbot under his arm.

Heads down, Kip and Finbar tried to run. But each step was like running through liquid concrete!

KER-**BOOM!**

The ground shook. Smoke filled the air. But the volcano didn't erupt molten lava. Instead, burning hot, electric-blue slime spewed all over the place!

Kip's spacesuit sizzled as slime shot through the air.

Lucky we've got our Cometchasers on, Kip thought, as hot slime gushed at his feet.

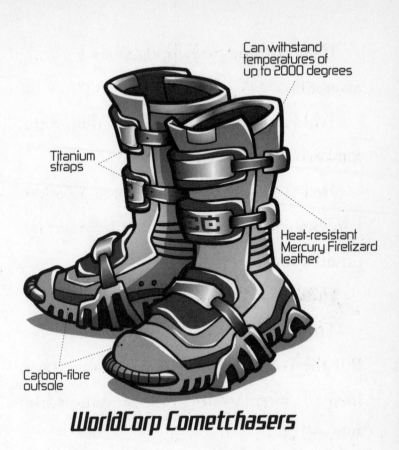

Can withstand temperatures of up to 2000 degrees

Titanium straps

Heat-resistant Mercury Firelizard leather

Carbon-fibre outsole

WorldCorp Cometchasers

Kip's spacesuit was heat-proof, but he wasn't sure how long it would last in the boiling slime. They needed shelter – now!

'Over there!' Finbar yelled. He'd spotted a rock ledge with his super wolf vision. The slime flowed over the ledge, leaving a space to shelter underneath.

Finbar dragged his feet towards the ledge, and Kip followed close behind.

Splashing through the slime waterfall, they collapsed in the large, shadowy cave beneath the ledge. Kip's legs ached.

Finbar's eyes adjusted to the gloom first. 'I don't think they've seen us,' he whispered.

'*Who* hasn't seen us?' Kip asked, following Finbar's gaze.

At the far end of the cave, near another entrance, a group of aliens was huddled

together. They were grunting intensely at each other and gesturing wildly at the blue slime.

The aliens were bigger than Finbar. They walked on two legs and had dirty, matted fur. Their curved fingernails were caked with scum. They looked pretty primitive to Kip.

Suddenly, Kip felt nervous. The last thing he wanted was to be stuck on a planet with slime volcanoes – and a group of massive, dirty aliens!

CHAPTER 4

Keep calm, Kip, he told himself. *Just because the aliens are dirty doesn't mean they're vicious beasts!*

Kip and Finbar ducked behind a rock to watch the aliens until they figured out what to do.

If Kip listened closely, he could just make out the grunts of the two closest aliens.

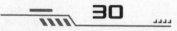

He switched his SpaceCuff to Translate mode.

Maybe I can understand what they're saying, he thought hopefully.

Translate mode used known alien languages to guess the meanings of new ones. It wasn't always reliable. But these aliens were speaking a simple language, and Kip could pick up bits and pieces of what they were saying.

After a moment, Kip nudged Finbar. 'I think they're complaining about the slime. But wouldn't they be used to it by now?'

'I guess they're sheltering from the volcano too,' Finbar said softly. 'The big one looks upset.'

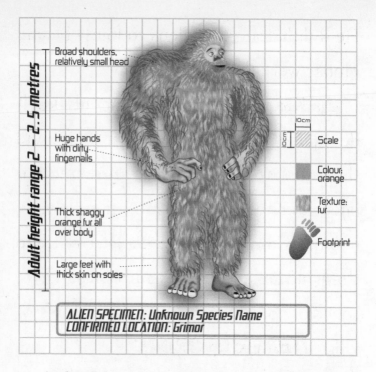

Adult height range 2 – 2.5 metres

Broad shoulders, relatively small head

Huge hands with dirty fingernails

Thick shaggy orange fur all over body

Large feet with thick skin on soles

10cm

10cm

Scale

Colour: orange

Texture: fur

Footprint

ALIEN SPECIMEN: Unknown Species Name
CONFIRMED LOCATION: Grimor

'I think her name's Zert,' Kip whispered to Finbar. 'That smaller alien there is her husband, Zorg.'

As Zorg talked to Zert, Kip followed his SpaceCuff. He had it switched to silent, so the translations were displayed as text.

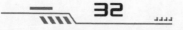

He didn't want the aliens to know he and Finbar were there yet.

As Kip watched, Zorg suddenly knelt down and hugged his wife gently around the knees. It was weird, but it seemed to cheer Zert up.

Maybe they're not vicious after all, Kip thought. *But they still seem a bit simple.*

Translate mode:

Grimor alien to English

Slime Pond...once volcano finishes... looking ...Slime Crawlers...

'I *think* they're planning on hunting something called Slime Crawlers when the eruption's over,' Kip whispered.

Finbar's snout wrinkled. 'I bet they're the things we saw in the puddles before.'

'The aliens must eat Slime Crawlers. I haven't seen any other food source,' Kip said.

Kip tried to keep an open mind about the aliens' strange customs. As a Space Scout, that's what he was trained to do. But he had to admit, Slime Crawlers didn't look delicious.

If Slime Crawlers were the only food source, Grimor wouldn't make a good Earth 2. And after doing a quick analysis on his SpaceCuff, Kip could tell the air wasn't safe to breathe either.

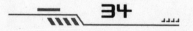

The reasons why humans couldn't live on Grimor were mounting fast. Kip explained his thinking to Finbar.

'Let's call MoNa and get going,' Finbar suggested softly.

Somehow, Kip felt sad to leave without knowing more about the aliens. They did seem interesting — just very grubby. But it was time to go home.

He tried to call MoNa on his SpaceCuff.

Communicate mode:

Satellite Signal: None

'My signal is blocked for some reason,' Kip said, annoyed. 'We'll have to try

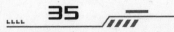

moving to higher ground to call MoNa.'

By now, the waterfall of slime had slowed to a trickle. Kip and Finbar backed out of the cave without disturbing the aliens.

Zorg was talking to Zert in an urgent voice.

'He's still going on about that slime pond,' Kip said, checking his SpaceCuff. 'Maybe they're going swimming!'

Finbar looked grossed out.

Kip needed to find the best spot for reception so he could talk to MoNa. 'I think we'll have to climb up there,' he said, after a minute. 'Even though it's an –'

'Active volcano!' Finbar cut in. 'We're NOT climbing that. It just erupted!'

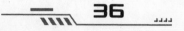

The Suckerbot spun its wheels nervously.

Kip shrugged. 'Unless you want to stay here, it's our only choice.'

In the high-gravity atmosphere, the climb would be tough and dangerous. And if the volcano erupted again, Kip and Finbar would be swept away in boiling-hot slime.

Luckily, they had their voice-activated Arachnalegs. These would give them vital support during the dangerous climb ahead.

Kip and Finbar started tramping heavily to the base of the volcano. When they got there, Kip engaged his Arachnalegs. All six suction caps stuck firmly on the ground.

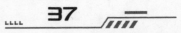

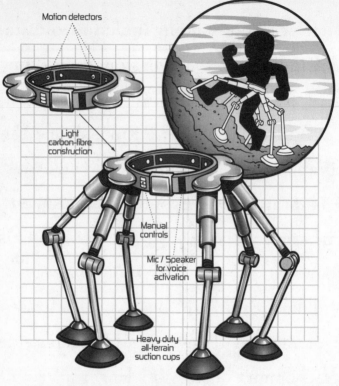

Motion detectors

Light
carbon-fibre
construction

Manual
controls

Mic / Speaker
for voice
activation

Heavy duty
all-terrain
suction cups

WorldCorp Arachnalegs

Then Kip started climbing up the
volcano, with the Arachnalegs supporting
his weight. Finbar followed close behind,
carrying the Suckerbot.

It was hard going up the volcano, especially with the high gravity dragging them backwards.

'Are you having fun?' Kip asked Finbar, trying to joke.

Finbar didn't answer. He'd stopped, tail stuck straight out the back of his spacesuit. *Uh-oh, that's his distress signal!* Kip thought.

There was an angry rumble deep inside the volcano.

'It's erupting again!' Finbar yelled. 'JUMP!'

CHAPTER 5

Blazing blue slime spurted from the crater. Kip and Finbar had to move or they'd be drenched!

'I'm falling!' Finbar yelled as slime loosened the suction caps on his Arachna-legs. He gripped the Suckerbot tightly.

'Me too!' Kip yelled.

SLURRRRRP!

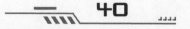

Kip was dragged down into the boiling slime. Luckily his spacesuit seemed to be able to withstand the heat.

'Watch your head!' Finbar roared.

Too late. The slime picked Kip up and hurled him into a somersault!

He bashed his helmet against a rock. His head rattled hard inside it, and then the world went black...

'Can you hear me?' whispered a voice.

Woozily, Kip opened his eyes. Finbar was beside him, looking worried. Next to him were the dirty faces of Zorg and Zert.

'They found us at the bottom of the

volcano,' Finbar said. 'They brought us home and nursed you.'

Up close, Kip could see that the aliens had friendly faces. He stuck out his hand for a handshake. Zorg took Kip's hand and patted himself three times on the shoulder with it.

That must be their version of shaking hands, Kip thought, trying not to giggle as he patted himself with Zorg's hand.

He looked around. He was in a spotlessly clean circular room. There was blue matting on the floor made of dried slime vines woven together. In one corner was a pile of plastic-wrapped bags of food. One bag was open. Kip could see some

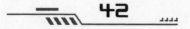

kind of dried vegetable inside.

So they don't eat Slime Crawlers, Kip noted, standing up. *But then where does their food come from?* The room swayed. Kip shook his head, trying to get his balance.

'Their house hangs in mid-air,' Finbar explained.

Kip wobbled towards the window. Outside, it was night. A bright green moon hung in the sky.

Kip could see two other houses shaped like beehives. Their tops were stuck to the underside of a rock ledge with dried sap from the blue vines.

'I guess they're designed to be protected from the hot slime,' Finbar commented.

Hexagonal windows
indicate advanced engineering

Houses attached to rock
using sap from vines

Grimor rock appears
to be similar to granite

'Slime runs right over the ledge and misses them.'

Kip knew these houses would be hard to build. Too hard for *simple* aliens…

Kip's stomach growled. He took a can of his favourite snack BurgerMousse from

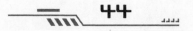

his backpack. He squirted some into his mouth through a hatch in his helmet. He then passed the can to Zert, who knew exactly how it worked.

She's done that before, Kip thought. *But there's nothing else like it on Grimor…*

Kip's brain ticked over. When he'd first seen the aliens, they looked dirty. Kip had decided they were a bit gross, and maybe even stupid. But jumping to conclusions was one of the worst mistakes Space Scouts could make!

He thought about the spotless, cleverly designed houses. The way Zert used the can of BurgerMousse so easily.

They're actually quite advanced! Kip

thought. He was annoyed for getting things so wrong. *But why are there so few of them?*

'Where are the rest of your people?' Kip asked.

Zert looked out the window and pointed towards the green moon. A tear rolled down her face. The aliens had funny hugs and handshakes. But tears meant the same thing all over the universe.

Kip was sure he could guess the sad truth. 'I think Zorg and Zert come from Grimor's moon,' he said quietly to Finbar. 'Judging by their provisions, they might have been on a short mission to explore Grimor, just like us!'

'Why are they still here?' asked Finbar.

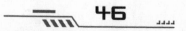

'Problems with their spacecraft?'

Kip turned to Zorg. 'Did you crash here?'

Zorg nodded glumly. He began to explain the aliens' story. Kip set the Space-Cuff to translate aloud this time so Finbar could hear.

'Our transporter was small. We crashed into a river of slime and it was carried away. We've searched Grimor but can't find the wreckage. The only place left is the Slime Pond near Pustula, the giant volcano.'

They said they were searching the Slime Pond before, Kip thought. *They must have been looking for their transporter, not hunting Slime Crawlers to eat!*

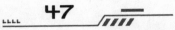

'We could take you home,' Kip offered.
'You could come in our starship, MoNa.'

Zorg and Zert grinned.

MoNa hated giving anyone lifts, but Kip didn't care. He tried to call her on his SpaceCuff again.

Communicate mode:

Satellite Signal: None

'Still no reception!' Kip said to Finbar, his stomach lurching.

'Maybe the slime damaged the Space-Cuff's satellite receiver,' Finbar replied. 'To fix it, a Technobot will have to totally rebuild it.'

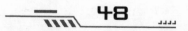

'Well, we don't have one of those here,' Kip said grimly. 'And if we can't call MoNa, we're trapped on Grimor. Just like Zorg and Zert!'

CHAPTER 6

'There's got to be a way to find your transporter!' Kip said to Zorg and Zert, and the SpaceCuff translated.

Zorg replied. 'We think our transporter is at the bottom of the Slime Pond. But we don't have any diving gear.'

'We do,' said Kip with a grin. 'Come on, let's go!'

At the door of Zert and Zorg's house, there was a rope made of knotted dried slime vines, hanging down to the ground. Kip climbed down from the hanging house, using the rope's knots as footholds.

Finbar, Zorg and Zert followed. Zorg called out to the other two houses. Four more aliens appeared and climbed down to help.

'Pustula's that way,' Finbar said, pointing.

Together, they all set off.

In Grimor's high-gravity atmosphere, trekking to the Slime Pond was exhausting. Beads of sweat popped up under Kip's helmet.

Kip saw the aliens staring at his

sweaty face. They weren't sweating at all. Kip guessed that they might not have sweat glands. To them, the sight of Kip's wet forehead probably looked bizarre.

Just like the way their handshake looks weird to us, Kip thought.

The aliens were clearly used to high gravity. Zert explained that the gravity on Zorn, Grimor's moon, was even higher than on Grimor.

Kip knew humans could never survive for a long time in a place like Zorn, no matter how friendly the locals were. It was hard enough to move around on Grimor, even for a super-fit Space Scout!

At last they came to Pustula's massive

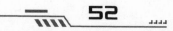

base. They circled it until they came to a large pond filled with cool, thick slime. The pond gave off a strong smell, like mouldy washing.

'The transporter could be at the bottom of the pond,' Finbar said. 'And we have no idea how deep it is.'

We're just going to have to search until we find it! Kip thought, determined.

He pulled his SecondSkin out of his backpack. SecondSkins were thin water-proof covers that fitted perfectly over spacesuits and helmets. They transformed any spacesuit into a diving suit.

Now, time to engage my CatsEyes!

CatsEyes were WorldCorp's latest and

coolest gadget. Flexible and ultra-light, they were radar contact lenses that Kip and Finbar wore under their eyelids. With a precise sequence of blinks, they could pop the CatsEyes down over their eyes whenever they needed to.

There would be no light under the slime. Instead, the CatsEyes would create a radar image inside Kip and Finbar's visors. Then they could see what was around them.

Finbar handed the Suckerbot to Zorg. At once, the other aliens crowded around, oohing and ahhing. They wanted to have a good look at the robot.

With a wave, Finbar and Kip waded into the slime pond.

It was gluier than a tissue full of snot. Unlike the hot slime from the volcanoes, the pond slime was very cool, and Kip shivered as they went deeper.

The slime was soon up to their necks. Kip and Finbar plunged underneath. It swallowed them up with a revolting sound.

GLUB GLUB GLUB!

Even with the CatsEyes, it was hard to see much under the slime. To Kip, Finbar was nothing but a wolfman-shaped blob beside him.

Reaching out, Kip grabbed Finbar's arm. He couldn't risk losing his 2iC in the slime.

Together, they dived deeper and deeper.

Kip's heart was soon hammering in his chest. The pond was much bigger than it had looked from the bank.

Kip scanned the pond-bed for any sign of the transporter.

For a while, there was nothing. But then he spotted an odd shape just below him. Round and flat, it was perfect for whizzing the short distance between Zorn and Grimor. It could be the transporter!

Pointing the shape out to Finbar, Kip gathered the energy he had left and he and Finbar stroked down through the slime. Kip hoped desperately that he was right.

And then… *yes!* They felt metal under their boots. Kip hadn't seen anything made of metal on Grimor. This had to be the transporter.

Suddenly, Kip felt something else. The transporter was trembling beneath him.

It shouldn't be moving, Kip thought. *It's wrecked!*

Something ran across Kip's foot through the thick slime.

What was that? Kip thought.

The thing was heavy and pretty big.

Even worse, it seemed to have hundreds of creepy-crawly legs…

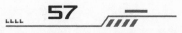

CHAPTER 7

Stay calm, Kip told himself sternly. As a Space Scout, he was trained to have superior control over his emotions. *There's some kind of critter down here. So what?*

Kip knew they had to take a closer look at the transporter, infested or not. Now they'd found the wreck, they had to work out how to get it out of the slime.

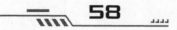

Kip and Finbar carefully crossed the transporter's flat roof. The metal was slippery and difficult to walk on.

Soon, Kip found something poking up from the roof. There was a hatch on top. He guessed it was some kind of airlock into the transporter. He forced open the hatch a little way and squeezed through.

Using the CatsEyes, Kip made out a ladder fixed to the wall. He climbed down nimbly into an airlock, and then inside the transporter itself. Finbar followed nervously.

This must be the bridge, Kip thought.

The small room was half-filled with slime. Six corridors led in all directions.

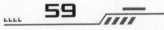

A can floated by, as though the aliens had been mid-snack when the transporter crashed.

Looking around, Kip could see through that the floor of the transporter wasn't quite flat. In fact, it seemed to ripple a little. He gulped uncertainly.

Finbar didn't seem to have noticed the floor. He pointed to the transporter's console.

Even coated in slime, Kip could see it was packed with dials, screens and navigation instruments. They weren't as high-tech as MoNa's. But it was extra evidence that the aliens were more advanced than they first seemed.

Suddenly, Finbar stopped. Standing completely still, his wolf ears twitched inside his helmet.

Kip's skin prickled. *I knew something wasn't right,* he thought.

AAAAAARRRGH!

Something made Kip trip up onto the floor. His breath was knocked out of him.

Gasping for air, he tried to pull himself up. But he couldn't!

Kip's ankles were tied together with some kind of thick rope.

Finbar stooped to help Kip up. But the second Finbar's gloved paws touched Kip's shoulders, the rope coiled around him too!

Desperately, Kip tried to tear his feet

free. But then he realised the rope had hundreds of moving legs attached.

It wasn't a rope – it was *alive*! The bridge was teeming with massive slimy creatures.

Hundreds of them slithered around Kip's neck, trying to pierce his suit with glistening fangs. And Finbar's arms were pinned to his side by even more of them.

Kip tried to keep his breathing steady, even though he wanted to scream. He'd seen these creatures before. It was in the slime puddles when they'd first landed on Grimor.

Slime Crawlers!

Back in the pond, they'd been tiny. But

the slime pond was clearly the perfect environment for Slime Crawlers. They'd shot up to hundreds of times bigger than their normal size!

Slime Crawler tails lashed at Kip's helmet.

Five eyes give more than 180 degree vision

Articulated body like a centipede's

Strong mandibles on jaw

Slime Crawler

There's no way these mega-crawlers will give up their home easily, Kip thought.

His mind whirred. There had to be a way to escape…

Suddenly, it came to him.

My UltraSonic Grenade! he thought. *It's in my spacesuit pocket.*

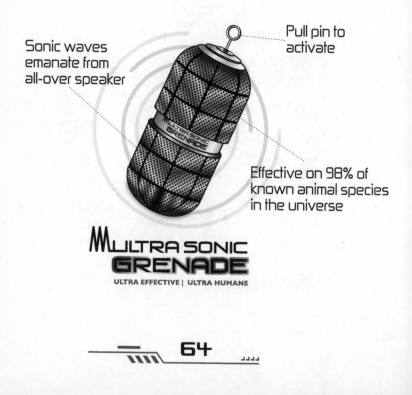

Sonic waves emanate from all-over speaker

Pull pin to activate

Effective on 98% of known animal species in the universe

ULTRA SONIC GRENADE

ULTRA EFFECTIVE | ULTRA HUMANE

The UltraSonic Grenade was a cruelty-free way to stop alien animal attacks. Pull the pin and the grenade released a squeal too high-pitched for human ears. But most animals found it unbearable.

To grab the grenade, Kip had to reach under his SecondSkin and inside his spacesuit pocket. And he had to do it covered in Slime Crawlers!

Gotta surprise them, Kip thought. He stopped struggling, and for a moment sat completely still. The Slime Crawlers seemed to slow down.

They must think they've got me, thought Kip.

Then, with a roar tearing from his

throat, Kip ripped off as many Slime Crawlers as possible. He plunged his hand under his SecondSkin. His fingers closed around the grenade in his pocket.

Kip yanked the pin, and there was a puff of smoke.

Immediately, the transporter began to rock violently. In a seething mass, the Slime Crawlers slithered away at top speed. They disappeared through the escape hatch and into the pond.

Kip couldn't hear a thing. But Finbar howled, burying his head in his lap. He was half-animal, so the grenade irritated his ears. Luckily, he had his helmet for extra protection.

Now to see if we can get the transporter out of here and flying again, Kip thought. *And then we can all go home!*

CHAPTER 8

Kip and Finbar swam speedily back up to the bank of the Slime Pond. Zorg and Zert were waiting there with the other aliens and Finbar's Suckerbot, which spun its wheels excitedly.

The aliens stuck their tongues out at Kip and Finbar, and wiggled them around, going cross-eyed at the same time. Then

they blew gigantic spit bubbles.

Kip was a bit taken aback. But then he remembered that these aliens had different customs. Although it was freaky, this must be their way of saying they were glad he and Finbar were back!

'We found your transporter!' Kip said.

All the aliens tapped their hands to the side of their heads over and over again.

Hmm, is that their way of clapping? Kip thought, frowning. He didn't want anyone getting too excited until he'd actually got the transporter back from the bottom of the pond.

Luckily, Finbar had a plan.

He picked up the Suckerbot and gave

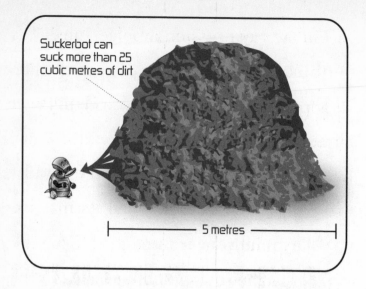

Suckerbot can suck more than 25 cubic metres of dirt

5 metres

it a little pat. 'This new model has an excellent atomic compactor,' Finbar said proudly, and Kip's SpaceCuff translated aloud for the aliens. 'It sucks up dirt and grime, and then shrinks down each particle to a fraction of its normal size.'

Kip looked doubtful. 'Can it shrink an entire pond's worth of slime?'

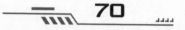

Finbar's expression was serious. 'It's our best shot.'

Kip nodded. 'I just hope those massive Slime Crawlers don't come back!'

Finbar led the Suckerbot to the edge of the pond. Eagerly, it plunged its massive nozzle-lips into the slime.

SCHLUUUUUP!

The Suckerbot slurped up the slime even faster than Kip could gulp a PlutoBlast Chill sports drink after a ParticleBall game.

Although it was only as tall as Finbar's knees, the Suckerbot seemed to find room for a limitless amount of slime.

The Suckerbot actually seemed to enjoy drinking slime! It made happy little purring sounds. Kip couldn't help gagging a little.

The minutes ticked by tensely. The Suckerbot was good, but could it really suck up the entire pond?

'Look!' Kip yelled suddenly. 'I can see the top of the transporter!'

The transporter's hatch soon poked through the surface of the pond.

Let's hope the atomic compactor holds out!

As he watched, Kip gave a nervous cough. The aliens stared at him, amazed.

'What does that barking sound mean in your language?' Zert asked.

'Mean?' said Kip slowly. 'Er…nothing. It's called a cough. It's…well…it's…'

Kip trailed off. How was he meant to

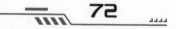

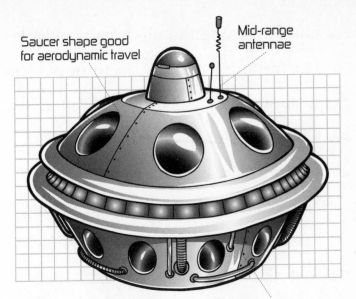

Saucer shape good
for aerodynamic travel

Mid-range
antennae

Alien Transporter

Suitable for short-
distance space travel

explain a cough to an alien? Coughs *were*
pretty weird, when he thought about it.

Suddenly, there one last loud sucking
sound. *Awesome!* The Suckerbot had
slurped up every trace of slime in the pond.
The transporter now sat in a dry pond-bed.

Kip, Finbar and the aliens hurried down to the transporter. The sooner they could get it going, the quicker the aliens could go back to their families, and Kip and Finbar could get home, too.

As Kip got closer to the transporter, a staircase unfolded with a loud groan.

That must be the main entrance! thought Kip. *It's a good sign the stairs are still working.*

The stairs were still coated with a slippery film of slime. Kip tramped carefully into the transporter.

With Finbar and the aliens close behind, Kip tore along one of the corridors leading to the bridge. Zert and Zorg explained to Kip that they didn't have experience in

repairing spacecraft. They were pretty new to space travel.

'Do you mind if I have a look, then?' Kip asked them, using his SpaceCuff.

Zert and Zorg looked grateful. 'Of course not!' said Zert.

Kip examined the simple controls carefully. They reminded Kip of pictures he'd seen of Earth's spacecraft back in the early 2000s.

Well, it should be easy to fly this thing, Kip thought. *As long as I can get it started!*

CHAPTER 9

Kip sat in a damp, slime-covered chair in front of the controls.

Zorg and Zert seemed happy to let Kip pilot them away from Grimor.

Kip felt around the ignition for a key. He wasn't very hopeful. After crashing into the slime, the key had almost certainly been lost.

Lucky I've got LiquidKey with me, Kip thought.

LiquidKey was the latest type of universal skeleton key. It was a tube of black putty. When squeezed into a lock, the putty hardened, leaving a little lump sticking out. The putty inside moulded to the exact size and shape of the lock. An instant key was created!

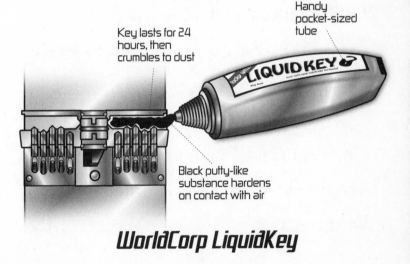

Key lasts for 24 hours, then crumbles to dust

Handy pocket-sized tube

LIQUID KEY

Black putty-like substance hardens on contact with air

WorldCorp LiquidKey

Only Space Scouts and top WorldCorp officials were trusted with LiquidKey. Without precautions, such a powerful tool could easily be put to the wrong use.

Kip squeezed a big blob into the ignition. When it had set, he turned the hard lump of putty that was sticking out.

I'm so close! Kip thought, crossing his fingers. *Come on...*

R-RRR-RR R R R-R-R

The engine spluttered, then died.

Kip suddenly felt cold and tired.

They'd chased away the massive Slime Crawlers. They'd found the transporter. They'd even made an ignition key! But all those victories were pointless if the

transporter wouldn't start.

The slime could be full of alien acid! Kip worried. *The entire engine might've been eaten away.*

Kip was trained in advanced starship engineering. He knew that major repairs could take days. Or even weeks, without spare parts handy – and there was no way to contact MoNa to get them.

He shoved those thoughts from his mind. He couldn't give in to doubt.

Kip turned the putty key again.

RR-rrr-RRR-RRRR

Yes! The engine fired! It just needed a few goes to warm up.

I'm used to MoNa's superior engineering,

Kip reminded himself. MoNa might have been bossy, but she always started first time.

Finbar cheered. The aliens did too, trying out an Earth cheer by copying Finbar. In their voices, it sounded a bit like ducks quacking.

Kip threw the gears into take-off mode.

The transporter was small and light. In Kip's skilled hands, it lifted off the dry ground and rose quickly upwards.

'We'll be back aboard MoNa in no time,' Kip said to Finbar.

Steering the transporter with one hand, Kip rested his feet on the dash. For the first time this entire mission, he relaxed.

'I'm not so sure,' Finbar replied quietly.

Kip followed Finbar's eyes. Through the transporter's slime-streaked windshield, Finbar was pointing to a slime volcano up ahead.

And not just any volcano. It was Pustula, the biggest slime volcano on Grimor!

A smell like curried eggs and minisaur farts filled the transporter. A plume of blue smoke shot into the air – and it was heading straight for the transporter!

Time to fly like never before! Kip thought, gunning the engine.

In Space Scout training, Starship Piloting was one of Kip's top subjects. But this time he'd have to fly perfectly. And he'd have to

do it in a transporter that he'd never flown before!

The slime plume spewed closer to the transporter, and Kip turned the controls sharply.

The transporter lurched left, sending Finbar and the aliens flying. The slime plume spurted right past them. But another one was heading their way!

Kip yanked the controls back in the other direction and stomped on the accelerator.

'Hang on everyone!' he yelled, as the slime plume hurtled toward them.

CHAPTER 10

The transporter tipped right and then flung itself upwards. Kip had avoided the slime plume by a millimetre.

'Nice work,' said Finbar.

Zorg and Zert tried the Earth cheer again. They were getting better!

'Just doing my job,' Kip said modestly.

Safely out of range of any more slime

eruptions, the transporter sped higher and Grimor's green moon grew bigger in the windshield. The aliens gazed longingly at their home.

With a bump, the transporter broke through the smoky atmosphere. Kip could see MoNa, but he couldn't talk to her. His SpaceCuff was still too gummed up with slime.

Kip switched on the transporter's communication beacon. In Space Scout terms, the tech-nology was primitive. But it would alert MoNa that there was a friendly spacecraft nearby. She could throw out a static line for Kip and Finbar to hold onto and spacewalk safely aboard.

But before Kip and Finbar began their short spacewalk, they wanted to say goodbye to the aliens.

Zorg dropped to the floor. He grabbed Kip around his knees and squeezed.

This hug is growing on me, Kip grinned to himself, and gave the aliens knee-hugs in return.

'It was nice to meet you, Zert and Zorg,' he said.

Finbar had a goodbye gift for the aliens. 'I thought you'd like to clean up before heading home,' he said, handing Zorg a SpaceShower from his backpack. 'I found it in my toiletry bag.'

SpaceShowers were tiny sponges flecked

with dirt-absorbing crystals. They were useful on especially grubby missions.

Zorg smiled gratefully. He held the SpaceShower to his fur. At once, the sponge sucked up all the slime and grime.

Underneath, Zorg's fur was soft, fluffy and baby-pink!

'They must have hated getting so dirty,' Finbar said to Kip, fluffing his own fur.

As Kip and Finbar left the transporter, the aliens pumped air under their armpits to make raspberry sounds. Kip guessed that was their way of waving goodbye!

Kip and Finbar bounded through space between the two starships. Kip loved being in zero gravity anytime, but after the high

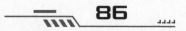

gravity of Grimor it was especially good.

When Kip and Finbar reached MoNa's landing bay, they tore off their helmets and breathed the clean air deeply.

Relieved, Finbar ran a paw through his fur. Kip could tell he couldn't wait to tidy up.

'No time for grooming,' came MoNa's voice from up near the ceiling.

'I know, I know,' Kip grumbled. 'Time to file my mission report.'

Kip and Finbar strode out of the landing bay and headed for MoNa's bridge. Settling on his captain's chair, Kip engaged his holographic consol. A screen was projected in front of him.

CAPTAIN'S LOG
Grimor

Terrain: A crusty, dirty planet covered with dangerous active slime volcanoes. High gravity makes it hard to get around.

Population: No permanent residents. Although we did encounter friendly aliens from Zorn, a nearby moon.

Animals: Slime Crawlers – gross and unfriendly local critters that grow massive in slimy environments.

Recommendation: I'm no neat freak but even I couldn't handle the dirt on Grimor. This place is definitely not Earth 2. Humans are not Suckerbots, after all. We don't want to spend all day cleaning.

KIP KIRBY, SPACE SCOUT #50

Phew, Kip thought. The mission was complete.

He hadn't discovered Earth 2. But at least he'd earn one Planetary Point for exploring Grimor.

Time to relax, he grinned. *First I'll play a bit of my new virtual hoverboard game, then...*

'I've just downloaded a message from your parents to my Galactagram chip,' said MoNa, interrupting Kip's daydream.

Uh-oh! Kip thought. *That doesn't sound good.*

Galactagrams were audio files, only used for urgent or extra important transmissions. MoNa's dashboard had a special chip for listening to them.

Guiltily, Kip remembered the time he'd wasted playing around with Jett's Pro-Planet Star Mic. He'd left his chores unfinished. His parents must be seriously unimpressed if they'd sent him a Galactagram!

Sighing, Kip took the chip from its storage slot in MoNa's dash. It was smaller than a pin-head. Kip rested the chip inside his ear.

His mum's voice filled his eardrum. 'I know you're busy,' she said calmly.

She's too mad even to yell, Kip thought grimly.

'And WorldCorp have just told us what an excellent job you did on Grimor,' his mum continued.

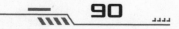

'We're proud of you, Kip,' came his dad's voice.

Kip's eyebrows shot up. *What?*

'That's why we think you deserve a week off your chores,' his mum finished. 'With full pocket-money. How does that sound?'

Kip grinned with relief.

That sounded better than hover-boarding, a jumbo can of BurgerMousse and a brand new Turbo RoboHorse all rolled into one!

THE END

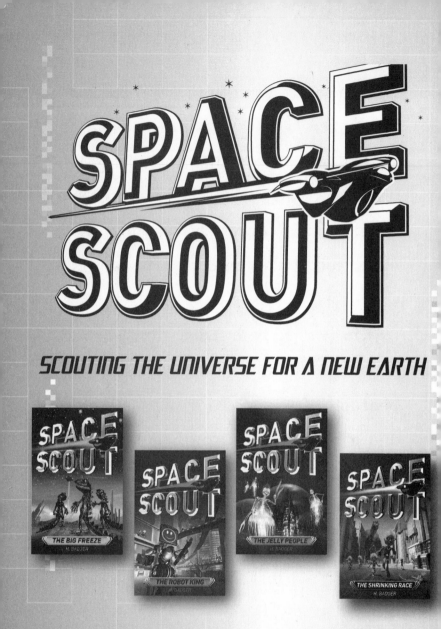